TINY'S
BATH

For M. and D.
—C. M.

To my ninety-five-year-old grandmother
Gaga, who showed me how to love laughter,
a good story, and God. I love you.
—R. D.

ISBN 0-439-13850-7

Text copyright © 1998 by Cari Meister.
Illustrations copyright © 1998 by Rich Davis.
All rights reserved. Published by Scholastic Inc.,
555 Broadway, New York, NY 10012, by arrangement with
Puffin Books, a division of Penguin Putnam Inc. SCHOLASTIC
and associated logos are trademarks and/or registered trademarks
of Scholastic Inc.

12 11 10 9 8 7 6 5 4 3 2 1   0 1 2 3 4/0

Printed in the U.S.A.   24

First Scholastic printing, September 1999

TINY'S
BATH

by Cari Meister
illustrated by Rich Davis

SCHOLASTIC INC.

New York Toronto London Auckland Sydney
Mexico City New Delhi Hong Kong

I have a very large dog.

His name is Tiny.

He is bigger than a bike.

He is bigger than a chair.

He is bigger than I am!

Tiny likes to dig.

He is dirty.

He needs a bath.

The pail is too small.

The sink is too small.

The bathtub is too small.

Where can I give Tiny a bath?

My pool!

Get the hose.

Get the brush. Get the soap.

Scrub, scrub, scrub.

Oh no! Watch out!

Tiny is clean. I am wet.

Stop, Tiny! Come back!

Oh no! Mud!

Tiny is dirty.

I am dirty.

Back to the pool.